PRAISE FOR M

The first...of (a) stellar, long-running romantic suspense series.

> — BOOKLIST, THE 20 BEST ROMANTIC
> SUSPENSE NOVELS: MODERN
> MASTERPIECES. *THE NIGHT IS MINE*

Top 10 Romance of 2012, 2015, and 2016.

> — BOOKLIST: THE NIGHT IS MINE, HOT
> POINT, HEART STRIKE

One of our favorite authors.

> — RT BOOK REVIEWS

Buchman has catapulted his way to the top tier of my favorite authors.

> — FRESH FICTION

A favorite author of mine. I'll read anything that carries his name, no questions asked. Meet your new favorite author!

> — THE SASSY BOOKSTER, FLASH OF FIRE

M.L. Buchman is guaranteed to get me lost in a good story.

I love Buchman's writing. His vivid descriptions bring everything to life in an unforgettable way.

AT THE SLIGHTEST SOUND - PART 3

SHADOW FORCE: PSI ROMANCE

M. L. BUCHMAN

Buchman Bookworks

Short Story Series by M. L. Buchman:

*W*hile rescuing Delta operator Hannah Tucker from the Colombian jungle, Jesse "Outlaw" Johnson makes a curious discovery. Hannah can create small sounds at a distance to distract the drug-running guerillas that are hunting them. And when they're in contact, he acts as an amplifier to that ability.

The problem? The louder the distraction, the more it takes out of Hannah. Her final outburst both saves their lives and knocks her out cold.

Doing their best to hide their new abilities during debriefing, Colonel Michael Gibson, the commander of Delta Force is not so easily distracted. Instead, he sends them to Jesse's hometown of San Antonio, Texas to contact the famous actress Isobel Manella.

Isobel has gifts beyond being a film star. She is also an empath—aware of others' true feelings. Her younger twin brother Ricardo is a former Delta operator who discovered the gift of telepathy, and it saves his life.

The catch, it only connects him to one person, his sister's old college roommate, the beautiful redhead Michelle. Michelle's half-half brother Anton, a towering black man and former US Army helicopter pilot with the ability to "see" places that are out of sight, completes the team that Gibson has sent them to meet.

Before Jesse's and Hannah's feet are firmly planted on Texas soil, they are taken aloft and over the border into Mexico. A combination of their six unique skills helps them extract a drug lord that the DEA has been unable to take down themselves.

That would all be fine, if that's all there was. But before Jesse and Hannah can come to terms with either their abilities or their deep attraction, another crisis is called in.

"*I* really hate this!"

Jesse pushed up on one elbow but didn't see one thing for Hannah to be complaining about. The horse pastures stretched away to the south and west: empty with the darkness and all of the horses being tucked in the barn. At the horizon, a soft glow marked San Antonio, the best city in Texas, which meant the best anywhere. But here at Daddy's ranch, it wasn't bright enough to dim the grand sweep of stars that he and Hannah lay beneath. They were swaddled up all snug in a couple blankets right on the edge of the sweeping prairie. Not wearing a stitch of clothing next to a woman like Hannah Tucker definitely kept him out of a complaining frame of mind.

"Other than making love to you, it looks like an idyllic night."

"*Other than?*" She was so cute when she got bristly. Of course, what with her being a Delta Force operator, he wouldn't be pointing the cute part out to her.

"Yep! Other than."

"Other than I'm gonna have to bury you in the deep cotton until you grow some manners?" Her smooth Tennessee accent and looking more than a little like Reese Witherspoon wasn't hurting things none either.

"That cotton would sure grow fine if you did. See, the real problem with you, Hannah—"

"*I'm* the problem, cowboy? Careful, you're walking on mighty thin ice here."

"It's May in Texas. Only ice we've got us is in a Coke or a fine sipping whiskey."

"Jesse," her growl only made him smile. He knew he was playing with fire, even if he couldn't see it in the dark, but he couldn't help himself around her.

"Would you like some? I could just trot up to the house and fetch whatever you'd like." He reached out and found his cowboy hat where he'd set it safely aside as they'd fallen on each other. He tugged it on, figuring she could see it against the sky.

"You'd go like that, buck naked?"

"Cowboy's never naked when he's got his hat on."

"But you're a US Army Night Stalker helicopter pilot."

"Second best hat a man could wear is a flight helmet."

Apparently having no answer to that, she returned to her earlier question. "I'm the problem?"

"Well, sure, Hannah. Think that should be plumb obvious."

"How?"

He pulled her tight against him; she only protested a little. "That deep connection thing we've got goin' on between us doesn't have a darn thing to do with idyllic."

4

"It doesn't?" Her tone had a smile in it. He never could pull a hat down over her eyes for long. "Then what would you call it?"

"Me?"

"You, Mr. Cowboy Jesse 'Outlaw' Johnson."

"Lucky."

"Lucky?"

"Sure. Like I must be the luckiest guy there ever was to have you lying in my arms."

For a time she pulled him in close, but he didn't have to be a horse-whisperer type to feel when her mind was still wandering off into the night.

"So, what's worrying at you, Hannah?"

"Why isn't it worrying at you?"

"I mostly just take things as they come along."

"Oh, so this crazy attraction between us, psychic powers to create and project sound, and Colonel Gibson sending us to meet up with a bunch of other psychics doesn't bother you at all."

"Nope. Though I admit *psychic* doesn't exactly give me an image I like. I asked Isobel about it while we were waiting on y'all to do that mission last night. She still thinks psi-chicks is the right replacement for psychics. When I pointed out that half of us weren't women, she suggest that *p-s-i*-s might work. Me? I find that awkward to say and far too close to, pardon my language, piss. Can't say as I like thinking of myself that way. I suggested psi-folk rather than psychic. But I'm not letting it get to me."

"Why not?" She was so close to begging that he forced himself to roll back enough that he wasn't preoccupied by

5

the feel of her.

"First off, I think that you're doing enough worrying for both of us and a herd of horses asides. Second, I don't really know enough to be worrying. I figure we spend some time with these folks, listen a bit, then maybe we can consider things all proper."

"Maybe it wore off in the night. After all, we only discovered it two days ago when I met you. Maybe I'm free of you now."

"Go ahead, make a sound. I dare you." Jesse scooped her against him. He jolted when an alarm clock seemed to go off hard by his ear—a loud one with the two bells on top and the clanger between them.

"I guess you heard that," she said on a sigh.

"My ears are still ringing. And you didn't hear a thing?"

"Still no." Hannah was silent for a long time with her face buried against his shoulder. "Do you really think it will be okay?"

"Wa'll," he thickened up his accent to beyond ridiculous. "I can tell you what I'm really a-thinkin' 'bout if'n you'd like, ma'am."

"Let me guess." Hannah snuggled in tighter.

"Good guess," he whispered as he buried his face once more in her lovely blonde hair.

CHAPTER 2

*H*annah felt surprisingly good as she sat at the breakfast table in the cozy ranch kitchen, despite her life being flipped all topsy-turvy.

Belle, a slender, cheery woman old enough to be Jesse's grandmother, clucked her way about the kitchen as she made eggs, bacon, and from-scratch biscuits with bacon-grease country gravy. If Jesse bringing home a girl was unusual, she made no sign of it. She served breakfast and embarrassing stories of Jesse's youth in equally generous portions.

Rather than blushing, Jesse would just tease her right back. The love between them ran deep and clear.

Terry Johnson's main contribution to stories about his son's antics were low chuckles.

Hannah had never sat a table like this one. Even before her pa had run off with Larry's wife and Larry, the abusive bastard, had moved in with Ma, it had never been easy and caring like this. A Delta Force table was either silent or they talked in low tones about mission profiles and the lame-ass moves of lesser forces, especially SEALs.

Even yesterday's BBQ dinner with the Manellas and Bowmans had been a soft and more serious affair. Not here in the Johnson household. She wasn't any surer how to react than when Jesse had held her close for such a long while in the night. Right out there. She could look through the kitchen's screen door and see where they'd made love. No. Had sex. She wasn't the sort of woman who made love.

Men liked their sex and done.

Jesse didn't have much to say, except when he was teasing her (something few got away with). Yet he seemed to think that keeping her close, after they were done, and watching the sunrise over the soft prairie lands was a good thing. She'd found it hard to complain even if she was just the next in some long line. He was certainly handsome enough to have his pick. His six-three of blond, blue-eyed, and soldier strong embodied the healthy outdoors look.

"So did Jesse just jump in the sack with a lot women?" The question just stumbled out. Before she could try to turn it into a tease, a deep voice with a Mexican accent spoke nearby.

"Oh, this is a conversation I want a part of," Ricardo Manella had slipped up to the screen door without her noticing—even for a Delta operator that was hard to do around her.

He knocked, then stepped in. "Hurry up, sis. This is gonna be good. Hello, sir," he stepped up to Jesse's dad. "Ricardo Manella, friend of these two here."

Friend? Hannah could count all her friends on a closed fist. The four other psi-gifted people who they'd met yesterday couldn't already be friends, even if she did like them. Of course she'd only known Jesse *two* days and, impossibly, they were lovers—she'd never taken one so fast.

Isobel stepped in, looking far beyond her mere beauty of yesterday. Ricardo looked much the same as yesterday, but Isobel had traded in her jeans and a button-down blouse for a flirty summer dress of deep red that revealed the 'movie star.' Hannah tried to remember if she'd ever worn a dress, but couldn't recall if she had. With how Isobel looked in one, she might have to find one to try out on the cowboy.

"This is my sister, Isobel," Ricardo's introduction was cut off by Belle's small shriek of surprise.

Belle clapped a hand over her own mouth, but it only muffled the sound.

Belle's reaction made Isobel's lips twitch—apparently being a famous film star had made her used to it. Belle blushed a brilliant red, mumbled out some apology through the hand she kept over her mouth, then hurriedly turned back to her stove.

Hannah was used to being unknown and invisible, and couldn't imagine being any other way.

Ricardo kicked out a chair and sat at the table. "We were just returning Jesse's lame-ass rental car—you really got to talk to your son about such things—when I overheard folks talking and came around the side. Must say, I gotta hear how Jesse answers that one. Give it up, Outlaw."

Belle had two mugs of coffee poured before Isobel even did her normal sigh at her twin brother's ways and sat beside him. Maybe if she didn't roll her eyes at him so much, he'd behave more. Though Hannah rather doubted that. Then she spotted Ricardo's smile just as he lifted his coffee mug in thanks to Belle. No, he knew exactly what he was doing to his sister.

"Pardon my little brother. I think he is still five," Isobel said with her perfect grace and lovely Spanish lilt in place.

"Nah," Ricardo replied. "Didn't get interested in girls until I was at least six. There was this one who got away. Denise," he offered a happy sigh. "She was the older and wiser woman."

"How much older?" Hannah gave him the expected line. She liked Ricardo, felt comfortable around a fellow Delta Force operator. In some ways more comfortable than she did around Jesse despite sleeping with him. Ricardo was the known—except for being a telepath. Jesse represented the unknown in so many strange ways she couldn't even begin to list them.

"She was seven. A whole year older, which is a lot when a boy is only six. Gods I worshipped her, but then she moved away. Broke my damn heart; never looked at a woman since."

"Ha!" His sister clearly knew how big a fib that was. Ricardo was darkly handsome with a dangerous look that Hannah knew a lot of women liked. She did herself…until she'd somehow stumbled into a far too wholesome cowboy.

"Okay, never looked at woman that way since." He

appeared to believe what he was saying. Isobel's shrug said that maybe that was even true. "Now you, give," Ricardo aimed a finger at Jesse.

"Wa'll…" Jesse stretched the word out to previously unachieved lengths.

Without being asked, Belle served up breakfast for Ricardo and Isobel. Ricardo slapped his hands over his heart as he looked down at the plate. Then he looked up at her. "If someone hasn't married this woman, look out. She's all mine."

"Thank you, Belle." Somehow Isobel had quietly learned the woman's name. Her kindness left Belle blinking in surprise for a moment, then she laughed at herself.

"Well if that don't beat all. You're downright civilized —not who I thought you'd be with all your on-screen antics. And if you were a little older, young man, I might take you up on that. But I don't need me a new puppy to train up. These two men were handful enough." As everyone laughed at Ricardo's pained expression, she served herself a plate and sat at the end of the table closest to the stove before continuing.

"Jesse was always a good boy. If he brought a girl home, he made sure that I had a chance to feed her a proper breakfast before he drove her back round to her place. But, as much as I hate telling the truth about the dear boy, he more often than not took them home after dinner and was home quick enough after. I expect he left more frustrated girls in this county than most other men. Boy is just too polite for his own good."

"Just tryin' to live up to your standards, Belle."

"Gowon," she flapped a fork at him happily.

Oddly, Hannah believed her. Despite how suddenly her relationship with Jesse had begun. Herself? She rarely slept with a man. Relationship logistics were hard for a military woman. Long deployments on short notice didn't make much of a chance for getting to know and like someone before inviting them into her bed.

Yet despite knowing Jesse for so short a time, she knew that what they had was somehow special—even if she didn't know quite how. Which was so freaking her out that she missed the transition from a busy table filled with laughter to just the four of them sitting at the cleared table, hunched over cooling refills of their coffee.

Isobel was watching her with those dark, penetrating eyes. "You're upset."

"I like you, Isobel, but I really don't like having some empath browsing through my emotions."

Her smile was soft and a little sad. "I'm not. It is a choice for me whether or not I can feel what you're feeling. If I was always wide open I'd have to go be a hermit in the desert—it feels like being battered when I open up near a crowd. But that doesn't mean that I'm blind. So, what's upsetting you?"

"It's not me, is it?" Jesse's made it a tease, but she could see that he wasn't as self-assured as he wished to be.

She glanced at Isobel. Was only reading emotions on occasion all she did? No, she'd said it was much more. Still, even if she wasn't "reading" Hannah at the moment, she *did* have a lifetime of practice matching faces to actual emotions with no guessing. So maybe...

Hannah sighed. "You're only part of my problem, cowboy."

"The good part, right?"

She traded a smile with Isobel; men were almost comical at times. "Yes, Jesse. You're definitely part of the good part. But it doesn't make you any less scary. But that's not what's bothering me right now. It's you," she turned to Ricardo.

"Me?" he grunted out in surprise.

"You left Delta. How? Why? And now you're a mercenary? That's just so wrong."

Ricardo nodded his agreement. The former Delta, SEALs, and Rangers who'd left the military, then joined the merc outfits, were just bottom rung.

Sure, the money and the adrenaline were a powerful draw, but… "Even the good ones are no more than guns for hire. Like a vigilante who takes bribes."

Isobel started to respond, to soothe, but Ricardo raised a hand to silence her.

"Yeah. I wrestled with that same shit. You know how hard I had to bust my ass to make Delta."

She did. Making The Unit—as Delta called themselves —was the hardest thing she'd ever done. And she sincerely hoped it was the hardest thing she ever *would* try.

"And I was good. Not one of the best, not like a Colonel Gibson, but I was damned good."

Delta weren't big on bragging, so if he said it, he probably was. "What happened?"

"What happened? I'll tell you what happened," he knocked back the rest of his coffee, slammed the mug down on the wooden table, and shoved it away. "I got in it bad, and deep too—pretty sure my ticket for this ride was punched and done. Then outta nowhere, there's this voice in my head asking me what's wrong. Asking if she could help. As if! Thought I'd lost my goddamn mind when this angel voice started talking to me out of nowhere— Michelle sounds just like in real life when she's telepathing into my head or whatever you call it."

Hannah wondered just how surprised Michelle would be to hear herself described that way by the apparently ungrateful Ricardo.

"I was hurting and figured I was hallucinating. Then her brother Anton spills blood getting me out of there. Fired a round of missiles from his Black Hawk to punch a hole in the jungle. Then he flew his damn bird right down into the hole, while the jungle was still burning and the guerillas were firing away, to come rescue me. Flew out with a round through his thigh and a crew chief who needed a new shoulder. I was too damn grateful to keep my mouth shut when Gibson popped up for my debrief— you know how he does."

The commander of all Delta Force had a habit of doing things like that. You never knew when he'd show up, he just did...and then seemed to fade away afterward without you noticing.

"This ain't no downgrade, sister. This is next-level shit."

"Doing an extraction for the DEA is next-level shit?" Sure, the ride-along mission she and Jesse had joined yesterday had taken out a major Mexican drug cartel leader, but it was a pretty standard op. Even if her "new" skill had come in useful.

"Yeah…about that…" But he didn't seem able to complete the sentence.

"This next one could be bad," Isobel broke her long silence. "We really need your help."

CHAPTER 3

"Is this your official office?" Jesse didn't know why he was complaining; the smells were incredible. But the first ribs of the BBQ Pit restaurant wouldn't be served for hours. It was barely after Belle's generous breakfast, but his stomach growled anyway.

They'd taken over the same table close by the big picture window with a sweeping view of the dusty gravel parking lot. The window needed a good cleaning; the scuffed Formica table didn't—it needed being tossed on the burn pile. The heat was already cooking up to a Texas May morning so everyone had a Coke or Dr Pepper with ice. A fan rattled away over the door, but it only added noise, not airflow, to the restaurant. A faded sign on an empty coffee urn announced, "Hot Dr Pepper December to February only. If you have a cold and want HDP out of season: Leave! We don't want your damn cold."

"It's run by an Army buddy's family," Anton explained. "Hard to find a better spot to be this side of San Antone."

"If he had it his way, he'd rename it San Anton," Michelle scoffed at her brother.

"Military City / Michelle City. I know how you think. You'd love it, Missy."

Rather than booting his knee, she stuck her tongue out at him this time.

The city was surrounded by two massive Air Force bases, multiple forts and camps, all joined together in Joint Base San Antonio—the largest joint base in the entire Department of Defense. The only oddity was that Jesse had ended up as an Army flier rather than an Air Force one despite being a local boy. Would he have been home more if he'd gone jet jockey? Maybe. Maybe then Daddy wouldn't have been so alone on the ranch.

He almost smiled. Hannah was a bad influence; now *he* was worrying at things. The Night Stalkers had kept him hopping about the globe, only rarely letting him get home to San Antonio. He'd hate leaving the Night Stalkers— actually, he couldn't imagine that happening—but he felt torn about wanting to be home more as well. Even just the one night with Hannah out on the prairie had made him so homesick he almost felt ill. Just as well the barbecue wasn't ready yet.

Isobel was watching him with curiosity from across the table.

He just shook his head. Whatever she was sensing, he definitely didn't want to talk about it.

Isobel looked at her watch. "I have one hour. Then I must leave. I have a shoot starting in Montana tonight."

"What is the sexiest Latina in film doing in Montana?"

"I am going there to kick a cowboy's ass, Jesse. You

think I am no more than this?" Isobel waved a hand at her face and fabulous body. "Don't make me prove it. Instead, think about who taught Ricardo how to fight." Her eyes were narrowed with a sudden anger.

"Delta Force, I expect, had a little to do with it." Quite what made him need to tease dangerous women, he wasn't sure. By Hannah's surprised glance, she didn't know either.

Isobel shook her head. "All they did was focus the training I had already given him." She thumped her bunched fingers against her breastbone.

"Wa'll. You might just have to prove it some. You said you're what makes this unruly lot tick. Let's see you do your stuff." He winked at her and she froze for a moment, then laughed.

"He likes living dangerously," Hannah explained for him.

"Just right for this crowd." Isobel turned to the others, who were debating which was the best of San Antonio's many nicknames.

Alamo City or Riverwalk City were no better than San Antone or Military City in his opinion. And The 210 for the city's area code was just plain silly; only surpassed by Countdown City for the area code's 2-1-0 nature. He wasn't too lazy to call his city by its proper name and he didn't know what everyone else's problem was.

"Fifty-six minutes," Isobel announced. "Then you're all on your own. So, do you want to keep telling stories or are we going to make a plan?"

That statement cut across the conversation with

enough effectiveness to show just how thoroughly the others had come to rely on her.

Ricardo made a few comments debating which was preferable, but Isobel had decades of experience in ignoring her twin brother and applied them now.

"I am so-o sorry to do this to you," Isobel turned to Hannah.

"But you're going to do it anyway." Jesse liked that her tone could dry clothes faster than Texas sunshine.

"I am." Isobel offered a graceful shrug of apology.

"AND HERE WE ARE," Hannah's sarcastic tone had not abated in the last seventeen hours. She knew it, but couldn't seem to turn it back off. Jesse crashing his helicopter in the Colombian jungle, just because he'd been shot down, had left her feeling equally untethered and also brought out her snarkiest side—at least snarkiest before this.

There, at least they'd been able to walk and fight their way *out* of the jungle.

Now they were taxiing up to the N'djili Airport terminal outside of Kinshasa, Democratic Republic of the Congo. As the sunset clamped down on southern Africa, she was still unable to judge exactly how this had happened.

"Camp Bullis Airport," Isobel had begun many hours and a number of time zones before, on another continent in another hemisphere, "lies just five miles that way from this restaurant. In forty-five minutes, I will drop you all there. An Army helo will be waiting to airlift you to Lackland Air Force Base. There's a Hercules C-130 on a cargo run to Hurlburt Field in Florida. Then a C-17 Globemaster III to Angola, and finally a civilian flight to Kinshasa."

When asked what was there, all she'd said was, "Remember Benghazi."

Nobody had needed another word.

A trumped-up riot, a Department of Defense reluctant to release Delta Force assets when and where they were needed (Delta had finally hijacked a plane to get on-site—arriving too late to save a pair of former SEALs turned CIA operatives), and the US ambassador to Libya (along with one of his aides) had paid for it with their lives back in 2012. Benghazi was a horror that didn't want repeating.

Hannah reset her watch to six p.m. local time.

And that simply, another seventeen hours of her life had just been spent in airplanes. The final leg—aboard a Boeing 737 that might have once been a decent aircraft but was now a 1960s miracle of aviation longevity that should not have been allowed off the ground—was landing them in one of the most dangerous countries in the world.

"What a place to come to," Ricardo grunted as the cabin door opened and disgorged them into the rampant heat and humidity. In those aspects, it was all too familiar. But the smells on the air, the ones that were strong enough to overpower the baking tarmac, were wrong. Spices of sweet BBQ were replaced with the hard bite of piss and rotting garbage. The gentle aura of unprocessed

21

sewage tainted the air briefly, until the sharp tang hit—
hydraulic fluid leaking from the sagging 737 onto the
baking pavement.

"Any bets on whether it will make it off the ground
again?" Jesse whispered in her ear. "Makes me want to
take a wrench to her and help her out."

"Makes me want to slap a breaching charge on one of
the fuel tanks and put the poor thing out of its misery."

Yes, less than two days out of Colombia, she was back
in the Third World. So much for her mandated two-week
medical leave.

"Jesse?"

"I know. Not exactly San Antonio, is it?"

"Not so much." He'd been as beaten and battered by
the long flights and numerous time zones as she had, yet
he didn't sound grumpy.

She knew she did. Her butt was grumpy from hard
jump seats and the final flight's cushions, tortuously aged
to neither look nor be comfortable. Her gut was grumpy.
Her head was very grumpy.

Most of all, her body was grumpy. One thing that any
spec ops soldier could do was sleep on a flight. A pre-
mission flight was the greatest knockout pill of them all.
Mostly because once they were on the ground and in a
mission, there was no telling how long it would be until
the next safe place to sleep.

Ricardo slept. Anton and Jesse too. Even Michelle.

But, except for minor catnaps, sleep had eluded
Hannah, even though she'd already been running short
from Colombia and then the Mexican raid and finally—
the only bright light in the whole thing—sex with a

genuine Night Stalker cowboy on a Texas prairie. And she no longer trusted her memory of that.

Had it even happened? It had blurred into all the other crap that was going on and now if she was asked for her name, she'd be double-checking her dog tags before admitting to even having one.

The one thing that the flight hadn't done? Knock her out.

"Remind me how we got here?"

"You got here because you're amazing, girlfriend," Michelle came up and slid a friendly arm around her waist. "I sometimes wonder what would have happened if I'd followed in Anton's footsteps. Maybe if I was lucky, I could have grown up to be you."

"Gone military? How are you at following rules?"

"Totally suck," Michelle admitted cheerfully.

"Then forget about the military."

"Ricardo said Delta is about *not* following the rules."

"Different kind of rules. Our job is to think about battle in ways that no one ever has. Whatever it takes to get the job done. Except half the time, some commander up the chain who doesn't understand what Delta can do will put all of these rules on what is and isn't allowed until we can barely breathe without betraying our orders."

"Wow," Michelle sounded awed. "Bitter much?"

Hannah worked for a smile but only managed it for Michelle's sake. "Never. Not a part of who I am."

"Uh-huh."

Well, Hannah had really failed to sell her that bill of goods.

"Bitter much about the luscious cowboy?" Michelle's

voice went low and implied all sorts of dark and nefarious acts.

Jesse had veered off to chat with Anton as they were waiting to be processed through customs, which appeared to be mostly about stuffing a twenty-dollar bill inside your passport. Or was the Democratic Republic of Congo forty for the passport bribe? Usually a briefing officer would remind her, but there hadn't been one in this case. She shot for a compromise of thirty and the official's delighted look as he emphatically stamped her passport said that she probably could have gotten through with a five.

Michelle, of course, breezed through with no more bribe than one of her angelic smiles and received an even more enthusiastic thump of the customs stamp.

Her question about Jesse was surprisingly astute—and Hannah was *not* enjoying the answer.

Jesse had crashed rather than rescuing her. He'd shot a drug-running jungle commando for putting on Jesse's dropped cowboy hat (and thereby ruining a perfectly good escape plan). He'd somehow become the catalyst for her previously unknown ability to project sounds outside her body and *then* revealed to her commander that she had some weird gift she'd never asked for…

Yet for these and other offenses, she wasn't the least bit bitter about him.

"I'm not a bitter person." Or was she? She hadn't meant to be—though her life had certainly been conspiring to turn her into one. A stepfather who enjoyed rape. A military that was trying to overcome its deeply misogynistic roots with only limited success. A command structure that spent more time being politically correct than effective. "I certainly don't want to be."

"Good. I don't want bitter girlfriends."

"I'll do you one better; I don't have girlfriends."

"Uh-huh," Michelle once again wielded her scimitar of disbelief. Then in answer, she slipped her arm back around Hannah's waist. "Tell that to Isobel. She already likes you a lot. And trust me. After knowing her as long as I have, if you weren't incredibly awesome—and she'd know—she wouldn't waste her time on you."

"Me?"

"Sure. This is Isobel Manella we're talking about here. Everyone wants a piece of her. You've never seen anything like what happens when she goes out in public. Even with her empath power, it's hard for her to know who she can trust. She trusts you; that's huge!"

Hannah was used to being trusted by her team, but not a whole variety-pack of other people.

Ricardo would trust her because she was Delta. Michelle trusted her because of Isobel and whatever weird senses Isobel deployed as an empath. Anton barely saw her because he was so enamored of flying with a Night Stalker. Jesse…

Jesse…just trusted her. From their first moment together in the jungle, with an entire phalanx of pissed-off guerillas storming down on them, he'd trusted her implicitly.

What the hell was a woman supposed to do with that?

CHAPTER 4

*T*he Chief of Station met them at the airport himself. That was never a good sign. When the CIA station was so small in a country that the chief himself was driving the pickup car, it meant there would be little to no backup or support—not that Jesse really expected any in a place like the Democratic Republic of the Congo. It also meant that anyone who knew the US's chief spook would now have their entire team on a watch list.

"Sorry," Chester Wilsworth apologized for the fifth time as he eased out of the airport and turned into westbound traffic, straight into the setting sun. "We're all a tad shorthanded at the moment."

"How long has *the moment* been?" Jesse almost wished that Isobel was with them to see if the station chief was merely pompous or both pompous *and* stupid. He'd cultivated England English manners, but the accent was wrong in some way he couldn't pin down.

"Current administration, I must say. They seem to think that diplomats and intelligence services have nothing to do with foreign policy. Everything now is all military this and trade-war that. Leaves all of us in a bit of a pickle."

"I think you've watched too much Monty Python," Ricardo called forward.

"Educated Eaton and Cambridge. My first posts were London at the old Chancery Building—ugly bit of work, that, and the new embassy is little better. The architect they chose…let's just say I've seen prettier war memorials. Sorry, I have a hard time switching off the old bonhomie. Sort of my trademark. Much like I suspect your cowboy is with that hat."

"He is beyond anything you can imagine," Hannah called from the backseat.

Jesse touched his black cowboy hat for comfort. He liked it even better now. Daddy had given it to him for his sixteenth birthday. Momma had woven the intricate hatband while he'd still been in the womb, not knowing she wouldn't survive his birth to give it to him herself. And just last night, on the Texas prairie, Hannah had become the first woman to ever wear it. He knew that the old adage about no woman wore a cowboy's hat other than his chosen one was just a bunch of hooey.

But a part of him didn't want it to be hooey.

At first it had been the sarcastic boots that had intrigued him—while he'd still been shaken enough from his crash landing that he thought her boots were doing the talking. Then there'd been little things, like her saving his life. But it wasn't even the deep visceral connection that he felt with her that had snagged his attention.

It was her.

He'd never met a woman like her and couldn't imagine he'd ever be lucky enough to again. The world simply wasn't the sort of place that could contain two Hannah Tuckers. Jesse was off the market and knew it as surely as Belle did when she'd hugged him goodbye this morning and told him how proud she was of him.

He never should have said he loved her. Hannah had been acting as if she hadn't heard that two nights ago and that was just as well. But he knew she had because he'd just blurted it out like a damn fool kid looking at his first pony. It had just popped out of him and there was no denying it.

Jesse glanced back at her, but she was now talking with Anton in the back row of the van. Michelle and Ricardo were in the middle mostly ignoring each other. He himself sat shotgun beside Chester.

The six-lane highway out of the airport, three each way, let them race along past crop fields for several kilometers. Then it was like they'd been tossed into a hard chute wall by a bronc.

The highway was no narrower, but after one yam field ended, the next one wasn't green growing things. The drifting dust and garbage along the pavement were unchanged. But suddenly they'd entered a vast shanty town of one-story hovels—which might be too kind a word for them. The roadway struggled along manfully for a few more kilometers as traffic poured in from side roads.

The congestion increased rapidly, the highway fast becoming less like a road and more like a stampede down a fast-narrowing arroyo with no gully-washer racing along behind to clean it out. It was narrowed to four lanes by the trucks that were parked in the outer lanes. Some appeared to be making deliveries, others were just eating their lunch. Their van struggled for at least five minutes as traffic compressed to one lane in either direction because apparently someone was selling decorative cellphone covers at a particularly good price and many folks had pulled over to make purchases out their vehicle windows.

"Not quite the Interstate," Jesse grumbled.

"Yes, Kinshasa is quite unique," Chester agreed cheerfully as he burst out the far side of the blockage and sprinted along for almost a hundred meters before the next traffic snarl—this time with no apparent cause. "This is lighter traffic than usual; you've landed on a good day. Since the great slaughter—"

"Slaughter? Can't say as I know much about the DRC."

"Oh dear," Chester sounded worried as he drove around a VW van doing the work of a forty-foot bus with perhaps thirty people on the roof and hanging out the doors, sometimes anchored by a single hand and foot—like a dalmatian puppy trying to pull the Budweiser beer wagon. "They had themselves a couple of civil wars here at the turn of the century—this century. One in ten people killed and all that. Five million dead, they had their own holocaust if you will, except the big killer was starvation and disease. Despite that, in the last twenty years the DRC's population has almost doubled. Kinshasa city has more than tripled in size since then—bigger than London, New York, or even Mexico City. Electricity, sewage, and what-not are all quite sketchy. Yet three-quarters of the DRC's economy comes from this city. Quite the hub of both the good and the bad."

Jesse tried not to feel ill. He'd seen enough suffering in Afghanistan and Yemen to last him a long, long time. And here was more suffering that he'd never even heard about.

"Care to tell us what's going on?" Ricardo thankfully picked up a piece of the conversation.

"As far as we can tell, same thing as was twenty-four hours ago." Chester slalomed around a cluster of delivery bicycles rigged with massive boxes and small trailers to tow along everything from a vast stack of rusting personal propane tanks to a couch.

"That's not particularly helpful, pardner."

Chester Wilsworth twisted away from watching the traffic to look at him and almost rammed a stray cow seeking new grazing grounds. "Hang on! Who are you people?"

"If you don't know, I don't think we're in a place to share. Who did you *think* we were?" Jesse held onto the door handle in case he had to bail out as Chester almost ran them into the side of a delivery truck that didn't bother even tapping its brakes before cutting into the traffic flow. It sent an unwary policeman scooting aside as if he had no purpose at all despite the small Stop sign he was holding.

"You're not SAD?"

"The CIA's Special Activities Division? No sir. Nor

31

your Special Operations Group. We're…" Jesse didn't know how to explain what they were.

"We're specialists," Michelle spoke smoothly as she leaned forward. "Perhaps it's safest for you if that's *all* you know." She ended mysteriously, but made it sound sincere. It was a good thing that Chester was too busy dodging a bus that was as crammed as the VW van had been or he'd have seen her teasing smile.

"Well now. That's rather curious, isn't it. Of course, if you can help us, I don't give a ruddy tinker's damn who you might be."

"All we know is the ambassador's in some sort of trouble." And one thing they'd all agreed on back at the BBQ Pit was that none of them had any idea how to help the ambassador if he was in *deep* trouble—which apparently he was.

CHESTER'S VOICE carried easily to the back of the van, but Hannah wished that it didn't.

"He what?" She turned from the dimly lit city to face forward. She couldn't have heard right.

"He went to Palais de la Nation, the presidential palace, five days ago to protest the president's latest abuses. He was also hoping to convince the president to ease ties with the Chinese…they account for over fifty percent of DRC export trade. Hell, they built the bleeding palace with a Chinese loan. Wait until you see it, it's a hundred meters longer than the White House, including the East and West Wings. No long breezeways either, it's a monster."

He went through describing what he knew of it: the open grounds, sitting on a grassy promontory pushing out into a curve of the Congo River that wrapped the presidential grounds on three sides. Brazzaville, the capital of the Republic of the Congo, lay two kilometers away directly across the river.

"They're still allowing Gordon rare visitors. He is under house arrest no matter that they use the words 'honored guest.' I've told them that you five are 'excited visitors' from his hometown."

Hannah looked around the van but no one was laughing. Was she the only one who got the joke?

"What's his hometown?" she asked into the strange silence.

She took stock. Six-five of black man and five-ten of redhead half-half siblings with accents that said New York. Ricardo's Tex-Mex accent far more sharp-edged than his twin's lush tones. A Texas cowboy and—

"Manchester, Georgia."

And Hannah could no more speak than breathe. Only four thousand people. She probably knew the ambassador's kids from school.

Someone else got the joke while she was quietly asphyxiating in the back.

Anton's laugh rolled out. "We got you covered if it was Texas, New York, or Tennessee," his friendly slap on her back restored her respiratory system to functioning even if her head wouldn't stop spinning. "But Georgia, brother, that's a serious stretch."

Manchester.

It simply wasn't possible.

She'd left behind mother, lecherous stepfather, her accent...her entire pre-Army life had been abandoned on the roadside when she'd stolen her stepfather's tricked-out Camaro, blasted into Atlanta on her eighteenth birthday, and abandoned it in the parking lot a few blocks from the Northside Drive Army recruiting station. By the time he'd reported it stolen, she'd already been signed, sealed, and delivered. Leaving the keys in it with the door unlocked had paid off as well—she heard later that someone had jacked the car that night and totally trashed it for her. It had probably been rude of her to call in and cancel his car insurance before she left.

If Ambassador Whoever Gordon had turned out to be one of Larry the Lech's drinking buddies, he could damn well rot in Kinshasa. She'd just keep a low profile and ride this one out. Just like she was doing with all this psi-chick nonsense.

In twelve days, she could cycle off med-leave, go back into the field, and forget about telepaths, empaths, flightpaths, and all those other paths. She'd get Gibson to assign her to the deepest darkest solo recon in history... and just never reemerge.

Except Jesse. What the hell was she going to do with a man who said that he loved her before he even slept with her? It was ridiculous. That was the only reason men used the word—not like they understood what it meant. She was no expert on its proper usage either, but she knew that much. Yet over breakfast at his ranch, Belle certainly implied that Jesse didn't play the field, instead being a straightforward kind of cowboy.

Which meant…

"Wait! Gordon? Gordon Delaney?" The name surged up from the past with all the subtlety of an RPG-7 Russian grenade launcher.

"Yes. That's the chap."

Hannah buried her face in her hands. She really didn't need this.

Maybe she was imagining everything. Maybe she was still safely lost near the drug-smuggling guerilla camp in the depths of the Colombia jungle.

She looked up between her fingers.

No such luck.

Instead, as Chester Wilsworth lurched to a halt, she was looking out the windshield at a giant traffic robot. Bright silver metal more than a story tall, it towered over the exact center of the intersection. It had a bright red light in the center of its chest and its arms were extended straight toward them. Traffic cameras for shoulder epaulettes looked sideways and cool sunglasses that probably hid two more cameras seemed to stare straight at her.

"What the hell!"

It raised its arms, twisted at the waist, and then lowered its arms again. Now it revealed that both the palm and the back of its hands were covered in green LEDs and the red lights on its chest and back were now facing the other direction of traffic.

"Aren't they simply splendid? A local woman thought them up and produces them. The Kinshasans pay no attention to the police, but we adore our traffic robots, so we always stop when they say to."

Hannah buried her face again. The robots were so bizarre that finding Gordon Delaney was the ambassador here seemed somehow inevitable rather than surreal.

CHAPTER 5

"*S*o we just walk in? Someone please tell me we have a better plan."

The sun had fully set and darkness was firmly clamped down on the dim city in the time it had taken them to fight the twenty-five kilometers from the airport to the Palais de la Nation. Streetlights were nonexistent in Kinshasa and it was only shop lights and the slashes of headlights that lit the streets at all. The massive crowds of the city churning along the street edges and shopfronts weren't present here. The plaza where Chester had dropped them off in front of the president's palace was a surprising sea of tranquility.

Jesse looked up at the towering bronze of the chubby Laurent Kabila that commanded the plaza. Kabila had become the nation's third president by bloody coup, overthrowing a three-decade dictatorship.

In turn, Kabila oversaw a massively corrupt and bloody regime until he'd been gunned down by one of his bodyguards. Rule passed on to his son, who managed to stretch two five-year terms into an equally bloody eighteen-year rule.

Despite the recent election of a new president—who had won the election under very suspicious circumstances —the lionized third president still loomed above them in portly bronze. As Chester had dropped them off, he'd pointed out that the body was rumored to be that of Kim Jong Il with a curiously Asian-faced Kabila bust put on top.

The North Koreans' most successful export was propaganda, often in the form of bargain-rate massive statues of African dictators who all looked suspiciously Korean. Jesse recalled one crew chief telling him about a trip to Senegal. The husband-wife-and-child trio of the fifteen-story-tall African Renaissance Monument looked so Korean that it was sometimes called the Korean Renaissance Monument. It commanded the skyline of their largest city, Dakar. Senegal was such a patient society that they were more amused than angry about the family's features.

"Anyone have a better plan?" Ricardo grumbled.

"Yeah," Michelle stared up at the looming statue. "Go back to the airport and go home. You'd need a major armed team to take down this place."

"And Gordon would be dead before they even reached the gates," Hannah spoke for the first time since Chester had dropped them off.

"Gordon?" Jesse looked down at her in surprise, but she didn't meet his gaze.

"High school. Drop it."

Jesse wasn't ready for the sharp pang of jealousy that

shot through him. He wasn't the jealous sort, except apparently about Hannah Tucker. High school? He'd known nothing about where that had been or what she'd done there—certainly never had thought she was a Georgia girl. Sports? Theater? Nerd? Friends? *Boyfriends?* He'd fallen for a woman who, for all he knew, hadn't existed before the moment they met at his crash site in the Colombian jungle. That was…wrong.

"You and me, Hannah. We've got some catching up to do when this is over."

"So not," she whispered back sharply.

She couldn't have struck him more deeply with a hard slap to the face. So that's the direction the wind blew from. Well, he didn't need more pain in his life.

"I think—" Ricardo started.

"Well that's new," Michelle teased him.

"I think," Ricardo repeated firmly, "that Hannah is right and that's why we were called in. We're the only team that can walk in here, get past the guards who would check us for weapons, and still have tricks up our sleeves."

Jesse again looked to Hannah—and she still wasn't meeting his gaze.

"You're killin' this cowboy, lady," he whispered it, then wished he hadn't when he saw her downcast nod.

HANNAH DIDN'T WANT A PAST.

And she'd honestly never given much thought to the future. And now that she suddenly had both, she didn't know what to do with either one.

Focus on the moment! That's how a Delta Force operator survived. From this instant, a hundred different branches could occur. The president's guard could shoot them on sight or this could be a cakewalk. The US ambassador to the DRC could actually be the Gordon Delaney who— She couldn't go there.

The secret to survival was flexibility. How was she supposed to be flexible when she no longer was certain of who she was? Or even what she was capable of. Sonic blasts that knocked her out? What part of the real world did that have to do with?

The only path is through!

"Let's do this." Her voice sounded harsh even to her own ears, but she couldn't do anything about this.

"Cowboy, keep your damn mouth shut," Ricardo had taken charge and she wasn't complaining. "Even these boys will recognize a Texas accent from movies. In case the ambassador's guards have a good ear, who here can fake a Georgia accent?"

Hannah winced, but operationally he was right to ask. She shifted her tone, "Not just Georgia, darlin'. Ambassador Delaney's from the same tiny, shithole town."

"I don't know anything about you, do I?" Jesse's surprise sounded hurt.

She shook her head. He didn't. But then again, she didn't either so they were even on that one.

"Whatever the lady wants." He bowed ever so slightly and shifted without moving. He had been standing close beside her with Anton on his other side. Now he stood by Anton and a canyon lay between them.

"I—"

"We're going to be suspicious if we stand here much longer," Michelle pointed out as she leaned a friendly shoulder against Hannah's. It didn't make her feel any better.

"If we get separated," Ricardo muttered as they circled around the towering Kabila, "try to pair off: Anton with me, Michelle and Hannah together because I'm counting on you to keep Michelle alive—she's a noncombatant. Jesse, you can apparently operate your sound trick with Hannah from either group."

It made sense strategically, split the telepaths so that the two groups could communicate. But she liked the idea of being separated from Jesse even less than the idea of being with him.

"Jesse, stick by me," she managed as they waited to cross the Avenue de Lemera over to the palace gates. The guards were already eyeing them suspiciously.

He looked surprised and comforted at her request.

"We need a pilot with each team, just in case." She didn't know why she needed to slash at him, but it seemed that she did.

She saw the last of the cowboy disappear behind the Night Stalker shield. It was the first time she'd seen him do that—not even under fire in Colombia. Hannah hated it, but didn't know what to do about it.

CHAPTER 6

*H*er Georgia accent turned out to be pointless at the gate because none of the guards spoke English. Thankfully, as a former French colony, that was the language of business and Michelle offered a fluent charm with that impossible ease she seemed to bring everywhere with her. Hannah's own high-school French couldn't begin to keep up, picking out little more than the gist of the conversation. She'd operated almost entirely in South and Central America, which gave her strong Spanish and Portuguese, but she'd had little reason to go into French Guiana, the only Francophone country in South America.

But she was able to feed small bits of information to Michelle and hear her slip them in as naturally as everything else.

"We're big supporters of the Blue Devils soccer team."

Michelle didn't even blink at that, just spun it straight into whatever babble she was spinning.

"The Ambassador was a star striker all through high school."

Like so many African countries, soccer was *huge* here. They started asking her questions about his win-loss record and his best games.

Hannah hated that she knew all the answers though it had been over ten years in her past.

Michelle eased the whole team through the security arch of metal detectors and guards waving wands at belt buckles. All the while she kept them talking about high school soccer in rural Georgia as if it was the most exciting thing since stealth technology. It was as if she wielded a magical cloak of invisibility.

Hannah definitely needed lessons in how to do Michelle's thing rather than splattering her emotions across every available surface. She never used to do that. No one could read her...until the goddamn cowboy.

"I'm starting to think that you're the problem, not me," she whispered to Jesse as they were escorted along the front walk toward the massive Palais de la Nation. It was an imposing three-story structure with full-height columns running along the entire facade—like a cage. The high-domed center bulged toward them like the curve of the White House Residence, but the two wings felt like a vulture's, preparing to sweep down and crush them.

Jesse simply looked down at her. No sign of Jesse Johnson in his cold blue eyes. Without the cowboy hat, she might not have recognized him.

"My life made sense until you came along."

"Please accept my apologies, ma'am." And they were back to that.

"Seriously, Jesse," she stopped him with a hand on his arm and the rest of the group moved ahead without them.

He looked down at her hand. She jerked it away, just in case the scream she could feel building inside decided to burst out as some amplified blast that leveled the palace. Maybe next time the backlash would kill her outright instead of just knocking her out cold. Definitely not the way she'd ever imagined going down.

"I don't know what to do with all of this. Every time I touch you, it feels so right. Every time we make some amplified sound together, it shatters something inside me."

Some of the softness came back into his eyes and she had to look away, letting her gaze drift over the grounds.

"You said you love me, Jesse."

"I shouldn't have done tha—"

Hannah held up a hand to stop him. "This isn't one of those if-I-don't-know-what-to-say-then-that's-the-answer situations. I don't even know *how* to feel, never mind *what* I feel." She could feel him staring down at her from under the brim of his cowboy hat for a long moment before making some decision.

"Wa'll," the cowboy was definitely back. He took her hand and tucked it around his elbow. "Then I s'pose that we'll just have to figure things out as we go along. Somewhere along the way, we're bound to stumble on a chicken or an egg and then we'll know where to start from."

As they walked toward where the others were waiting for them at the front entrance, she still couldn't look at him. Holding on to his arm felt too good and she didn't know how to react.

Instead, she inspected the palace, as well lit by floodlights as the city wasn't. Radial paths reached across the daylight-bright green lawn all centered on the main entrance. A few low bushes drooped toward a browning lawn. A lone, unimpressive fountain splashed sullenly under the bright lights. The few trees didn't quite mask the utility buildings to the west nor the large service building to the northwest, backed against the Congo River. To the east was a very limited amount of parking and then the dark expanse of the river's bend with scattered lights of boats sliding along the current.

Due north, shining in a blinding white light, towered the massive edifice from which they were somehow supposed to extract the ambassador of the United States without getting him or themselves killed.

"This is going to be *so* much fun."

"Yep!" Jesse agreed happily, apparently ignoring her tone. "Lookin' forward it."

"You're a strange man, cowboy."

"Never been one to argue with a woman," was all he said as they reached the others and entered the building.

JESSE HAD FELT some sort of switch get thrown while talking to Hannah. It wasn't just that her least touch could remind a man how it felt to stand out under the Texas stars. It was more like finding an auxiliary hydraulic system kicking in after the primary had been shot out—suddenly everything was handling smooth again.

Hannah being afraid just didn't sound right for a Delta operator, but he hadn't been able to doubt the worry in her eyes. If she needed time, he'd give that to her—he *knew* how *he* felt. Yes, he didn't know diddly or squat about her past, but he knew what he needed to know— she was the woman for him.

Fine.

She needed help figuring that out for herself?

Again fine.

He was the man to do it. Daddy had always said that the first time he met Momma, he just knew she was the only one for him.

And Jesse now knew that was true. It had worked for Daddy, and by God, it was going to work for him. No US ambassador was going to get the better of him again. He had taken Jesse for a short ride off the trail there, but he'd found his way back. Just had to help Hannah guide herself to the same path was all.

The front doors looked as if they belonged to a shopping mall. For all the columns and pomp, the designer clearly had no imagination. And...yep. As he suspected, the first room was a vast space meant to intimidate through sheer size, but not by elegant design. Massive press conferences could be held beneath the three-story-up dome. But it had none of the charm that he'd seen in pictures of the White House. The walls had the flatness of concrete. The space was too big, despite the few bits of art and statuary put in, to feel anything other than empty.

The three heavily armed escorts were still chatting happily with Michelle as they led them up a staircase and out onto a second-story balcony that ran along the outside of the entire face of the building.

Through the massive colonnade on their left, the city pulsed in the night. A section of it was pitch dark; the kind of darkness that only comes from a power-grid failure. Even as he watched, it flickered on, stuttered, then crashed back into blackness, taking the section of the city next to it down into blackness as well. The sweep of lawn in front of the palace was still blindingly lit. He'd wager that the president's home was never without power—ever. He also noted they were too high to jump safely. Access to stairs would be a high priority for the mission.

On their right, a series of rooms opened off the walkway. A few were offices, but most were dark and appeared to be rooms more appropriate for a museum. How much of the country's riches were stashed away in these rooms accessible only to the president's inner circle? Most would be his bet.

He focused on Hannah's hold on the crook of his arm. It was hard not to as she was gripping him with a Delta operator's fearsome strength. What did The Unit do to their personnel that made them so strong?

"Maybe if you—"

Hannah cut him off with an even tighter squeeze and a curt shake of her head.

Perfect.

Their three escort guards stopped at a door where two more guards were posted.

Five and counting.

CHAPTER 7

*H*annah forced herself to relax. She could see Ricardo doing the same. Hopefully the DRC's soldiers weren't trained well enough to see it. It was one of the secrets of Special Operations. Jesse would know it, of course. Only from a place of ease was the maximum flexibility of action possible. All senses on alert. Body relaxed and flexible.

None of that was going to help with Ambassador Gordon Delaney.

With an apologetic squeeze of Jesse's arm, she let go of him and shifted so that she was at the ready for anything.

Out of the corner of her eye, she could see Jesse flexing his arm as if trying to get circulation back. She flexed her fingers and realized they were sorer than after firing a couple hundred rounds. No time to apologize now.

The guards knocked, opened the door, and let them in.

They shut the door behind them. She heard the lock snick into place.

The room was a spacious all-in-one, lit by a few scattered lamps. A gray leather couch with a leopard skin throw—that was probably real leopard—commanded a small seating area. The spotted throw was only the first element of a common theme. An elephant's head complete with tusks dominated one wall. She looked back at the couch and realized it was made of elephant-skin leather. Other trophies large and small were mixed in with native woodcarvings of strange heads and stranger animals.

A dining table had been co-opted into a desk, evidenced by the ambassador's briefcase and a few pads of paper. A large bed faced a window at the far side of the room. Beyond it lay the bright lights of Brazzaville over in the Republic of the Congo across the broad reach of the Congo River.

She almost felt a smile remembering her swim with Jesse in the crocodile-infested Naya River. That now seemed so trivial, even safe by comparison. She tried not to estimate the likelihood of their bodies floating down the Congo River before the night was over.

This is just recon, she reminded herself. Nothing more. From this, they'd build a plan of attack. At the moment they were just fans from home.

From home.

A home she'd done everything in her power to erase from her memory.

And succeeded until—

"Hanners?" Gordon walked toward them out of the shadows at the far side of the room. "Sweet Jesus, never thought I'd be so glad to see your face." Without hesitation, he stepped up and wrapped his arms around her like they were long-lost friends rather than mortal enemies related by...whatever they were related by. His father Larry and her ma had never divorced their former runaway spouses, just lived in sin—in so many ways.

"Hey, Gordon," somehow she kept her voice even.

"What the hell are you doing here?"

"You tell me."

"I've been kidnapped into this luxury jail by the president for implying that the US would sanction his country severely if he didn't break with his predecessor's policies. Now answer my question."

She didn't feel the creepy crawlies she'd expected. Gordon had been home so little through high school. Between academics, soccer, and his friends, there were times she didn't see him *except* at school for weeks.

"Did your ma send you? You seen her lately?"

"Are you kidding me? So she can let your father rape me some more?"

"He *what!*" His voice was echoed by Jesse in his black cowboy hat who suddenly stepped forward until they were both crowding Hannah. She tried to step back from Gordon's confusion and Jesse's black rage, but just trod hard on someone's toes.

"I'm so sorry, girlfriend," Michelle whispered in her ear as she rested a hand on Hannah's shoulder from behind.

"Look," Anton stepped forward. "We don't have time for happy family reunions. We're on the clock here."

"What are you talking about?" Even Gordon, who had

always towered over her, appeared small when he faced Anton. Then he turned to her, "What's he talking about?"

"Ricardo says we're running out of time really fast," Michelle whispered again. "Some officer just came up in a hurry. I've really got to teach Ricardo French. He can hear them but can't understand a word."

Hannah scanned the room and saw that Ricardo was still close by the front door. Telepathy. Right. He was silently updating Michelle. That was going to take some getting used to.

Unable to think of what else to do, she grabbed Jesse's arm. That instant of contact surged through her. Not loudly, but enough to be heard, she imagined knocking on the inside of the doors to either side of the ambassador's room.

"They're moving off. Did you do something?"

Hannah nodded just enough that only Michelle standing so close would notice. Then she held up pinched fingers to show that what she'd done wasn't going to last long.

"Gordon? What are the ways out of here?"

"What. Are. You. Doing. Here?"

He'd always been stone stubborn. Maybe that's what you had to be to pull off being an ambassador. "We're a special squad sent in to extract you."

"You're military? Is that what happened to you?"

"Gordon. Focus. Now."

"But—"

Hannah wasn't ready for what happened next.

Six-three of blond cowboy took six-one of brunette ambassador by his lapels, lifted him in the air, and shook him hard. "If you don't start paying attention to what Hannah says when she says it, you and I are going to have a problem, pardner. And that problem is gonna start with me tossing you to the dogs as a bone while our team gets our asses back out of here. Are we clear now?"

"Now, Hannah," Michelle's whisper was hurried.

Hannah stood for a moment longer, mesmerized by this new side of Jesse. In the last few hours she'd sent him whole handfuls of mixed messages. Yet this was the first time she'd ever seen him truly angry.

Not at the guerillas who had been trying to kill them.

Not at her commander for refusing to let her sleep until she'd answered his questions.

Not about Mexican drug lords or being dragged into dangerous situations with too little preparation.

No.

Jesse was enraged because someone wasn't paying attention to her.

At that, another piece of the insanity going on inside her cracked.

There was a reason that she was typically an action team of one—because no one listened to a five-six blonde woman, no matter what her credentials.

But Jesse did.

"Now," Jesse still hadn't let Gordon's toes back onto the thick carpet. "Options other than the front door?"

"None. Back windows are all sealed."

Jesse dropped him down and he almost collapsed to the ground. He grabbed her arm and raced to the window. It was a tall second story down to the ground. The grounds were a wide, open area leading down to a high iron fence along the river. Small triangular pools surrounded a trapezoidal pool, murky with algal growth and providing nothing in the way of decent cover even if they could get there.

Ugly as sin besides.

JESSE WAS STANDING at about the same height above the grounds that he normally flew his Little Bird helicopter. The yard was well enough lit that Jesse easily picked out the four guards in the yard by their characteristic foreshortened shape when viewed from this height. Plus the five out front. Plus the gate guards and…

The four down below look bored out of their skulls, which gave him an idea.

"Gunfire," he grabbed Hannah's hand. "Nothing big. Just enough at the corner of the building to sound like it's coming from out front. Lead them all away."

"All who?"

She must be really thrown at the moment to not see the guards. He placed a hand on either side of her face. "I'm not going to pick you up and shake you, but you need to reel it in right now."

Hannah nodded, but her eyes didn't focus any better than a hoot owl's caught out at high noon.

He pulled her hard against his chest.

"Ricardo says they're coming back."

Jesse wasn't sure what Michelle was talking about, but didn't figure it meant anything good.

"Okay, honey," he told the top of Hannah's head and

hoped that the rest of her was listening. "We're gonna do this together."

Then, instead of imagining that he was just some sort of power amplifier for her sound capabilities, he did his best to pretend there were a couple sharp bursts of gunfire at the corner of the building. He felt it flow between them in some strange way that was both inside them—yet not.

Michelle twisted to look out the window as the guards reacted.

Three ducked and then raced for the corner of the building. The fourth dropped his rifle and bolted away in the opposite direction.

Jesse imagined more gunfire around the next corner. Then a little at the front gate and a final burst that would sound as if it came from the five guards waiting outside their own second balcony front door.

The last was probably a mistake. The gate guards apparently decided that his small party had overwhelmed their guards, stolen their weapons, and were now staging the first phase of a major rescue effort. With no plan and little care, the gate guards fired at the guards still clustered on the front balcony outside the room.

Ricardo yelped and dove for the floor as a stream of bullets blew in the front windows.

"He isn't hurt," Michelle reported as the bullets, fired from below, slammed into the ceiling, raining dust and plaster chips down on everyone. "He just squeals like a little girl when people shoot at him."

If he sent back any wry laughter, she didn't repeat it.

Their own guards began firing back.

Anton stood like a statue for a long moment until Michelle managed to tug him down to kneeling. "Three-way battle. Front gate, balcony, and the three guys hunkered at the corner." His eyes glazed over for a moment more. "More guards coming out the front doors of the palace. There's some firing along the perimeter fences as well. Guess we aren't going back out the way we came in. What's the plan, Jesse?"

"Jesse? Me? You think I have a plan?"

"You or me, boss. Ricardo's still over there."

Jesse glanced around just in time to see Ricardo land a flying tackle on the ambassador just as someone got a better angle and more bullets flew into the room, striking lower on the walls.

"Hit the window," Jesse told Anton.

"With my fist? No thanks, man."

"Try a chair, big guy," Michelle dragged one over.

Anton heaved the chair at the window facing the river and it bounced off. "Dude put bulletproof glass on this side, but not on the side facing the gate? Not real smart."

Hannah had recovered enough to reach out and lay a hand on the glass. He heard the same sliding set of sounds Hannah had used to find the vibration to break down the mortar of the Mexican drug lord's hacienda.

"Nothing," he didn't need to see her shake her head to know it hadn't worked.

"Duck!" Michelle shouted out and they both hit the ground.

Anton called out, "Sorry, buddy!" just as he heaved something massive at the window.

It blew outward. The pane didn't break, it just bowed

enough to pull it out of all of its molding all the way around.

Jesse peeked over the edge and looked down below, then he started to laugh. "Y'all be careful when you jump."

Anton had heaved the massive mounted elephant's head through the window. It had landed on it neck so that it faced upward and its tusks were pointed straight up into the air.

Michelle yanked the sheets off the big bed and tied their corners together. She handed one end to Ricardo, who barely had time to grab hold before she was out the window and sliding downward, trusting him completely.

"I guess we're rescuing you *now*," Hannah shoved Gordon toward the window hard enough that he almost went out over the sill, then she and Jesse followed him down with Anton right behind.

Jesse still didn't get what was going on with Gordon, but Jesse wasn't letting her go anywhere without him at her side until they straightened that out. If the ambassador had anything to do with someone molesting Hannah, he would kill the man himself and screw the rescue.

Ricardo was the last down—he'd tied off the bedsheet to something inside, but it got him close enough to the ground that he could jump safely without impaling himself.

"Anton. What's in that building?" Hannah pointed at a large building on the edge of the property.

Jesse hadn't noticed it before. Couldn't imagine why Hannah cared… Until he saw the doors.

Hangar doors.

No runway. Maybe the president's personal escape helicopter was parked in there.

"Oh, baby," Anton's low statement of delight was all that Jesse needed to hear.

JESSE FLEW the Chinese Changhe Z-11 helicopter, which fortunately had six seats, smoothly southeast.

Hannah watched out the side window as he followed the Congo River—but from the Republic of the Congo's side. No one appeared to have noticed their departure.

Gordon had explained what they might face during their escape. "The DRC doesn't have an air force as such that they can scramble. A few old Russian helicopters, only the Mil Mi-24 gunships would be a real threat, but they're all engaged in the east. Six old jets that I don't think are functional anymore. A Boeing 737 fitted out for VIP transport of the president. That's it. He must have traded with the Chinese for this little number at some point. I expect that he kept it close at hand in case he had to escape a coup."

"Not a single shot fired on DRC soil by US forces," Ricardo high-fived her at that.

"How *did* you do that?"

Ricardo hemmed and hawed and Hannah didn't have a much better answer.

"I'm sorry, sir," Michelle offered brightly. "That's classified."

"Classified?" Gordon scowled, then he turned on

Hannah. "You went into the military? Is that what happened to you? One day you just disappeared."

Hannah nodded.

"To get away from…" He had the decency not to name his own father.

She nodded again.

"I'd kill the goddamn bastard if he wasn't already dead."

"He's dead?" It was like another piece of the world had slipped out from under her and she was skating on the nonexistently thin Texas ice.

"Killed himself. At least that's how they ruled it. Pretty sure your ma helped him along the way. She's with another guy…not all that much better, I guess."

Hannah was only surprised that her mother had thought it worth standing up for herself even once—she'd certainly never done so for her daughter. Larry was dead. The world had just become a better place; not that she'd ever be going back to Manchester, Georgia, anyway.

"You never did talk much, Hanners. Guess I know a bit of why now."

Ricardo opened his mouth, but Michelle elbowed him sharply. He scowled at her, but he didn't try to say that it was part of being a Delta Force operator.

"Still don't talk, I see." Gordon shrugged. "I hope you'll stay in some touch with me, at least. I like being able to thank you for saving my life."

She shrugged back a maybe. She'd have to think about that.

They flew in silence until they were out to sea and a waiting aircraft carrier was already in plain view.

"You know," Gordon smiled at her, then slipped into a deep Georgia accent that he'd removed from his voice even more effectively than she had. "Pa was hellfire pissed when his Camaro went missing about the same time you did. Don't s'pose you know a thing 'bout that."

He didn't make it a question, so she didn't bother answering; but they shared a smile and finally traded phone numbers on the carrier deck.

CHAPTER 8

"*I*t's been almost two weeks since we first met in the Colombian jungle—one of us right side up and the other absolutely not."

"You always seem to make me feel that way, Hannah." Jesse figured it was like the first time riding a horse. Something he didn't remember, but Hannah had sure complained about it until she got the feeling that being in the saddle was better than sitting on her butt in the tall grass looking up at a horse. She made him feel all off balance.

They'd taken a couple of blankets and ridden out onto the open prairie. Their horses slept quietly where they'd been tethered on long leads near an old oak tree. The stars were out again as he held her close. He'd learned to leave Hannah lots of silence for her thoughts, so he just nuzzled her hair shining in the starlight and watched for stray meteors to streak across the stars.

"There are some things that need talking about, Jesse."

"Fire when ready, ma'am." She kept her silence, but he could tell she was just teasing him, so he blew a raspberry sound against the top of her head.

"Okay, okay. First, we made all those sounds—that knocked me for a loop and that everyone except me heard, which I still hate—but this time I didn't feel a thing. It didn't drain me the way it did in Colombia or Mexico. How?"

"I had me this idea, holding you in my arms as I was in the ambassador's room."

"And what was that?"

"Two things. First, you're Delta Force. You specialize in the small, tactical strike. I think that something like creating a little decoy sound just fits your nature and it was only when we tried pushing for big sounds that it didn't agree with you."

"I like the way that sounds. I actually like that a lot. What's second?" She began tracing ticklish circles on his chest with her fingertip and he wondered what she was mapping out.

"Second, I asked myself what would it be like if we were in this together? Instead of just me pushing whatever this is through you, what if we did it like we were one."

"Did it?" Her voice teased as she shifted where her hand was tracing. It made him catch his breath sharply enough to make one of the horses snort with sudden wakefulness. Horses generally worried about things like predators even more than Hannah did.

"It's a work in progress, Hannah. We'll get it figured

out," he managed when she once more lay quietly against him.

"Hmm. I like the sound of that too."

"There's a couple other things I like the sound of," he told her and wished upon a passing satellite because shooting stars seemed to be especially rare now that he was needing one to wish on.

"What're they, cowboy?"

"Isobel called. She wants the whole team to fly up to Montana. Something's going on, but she wouldn't say what. Just asked if we'd come."

"I'm supposed to report back to Gibson tomorrow and you to your team."

In answer, he held up his phone and woke it up to show her the finished, but unsent, message there that he'd addressed to Gibson.

She read it without comment, then rested her head back on his shoulder.

"Do you really think so, Jesse?"

"I do."

Hannah was silent for a while. "You said there were a couple of things, cowboy."

"Wa'll—"

"Oh brother. Here we go."

"I got you a small present."

She went quiet, almost all the way to Delta quiet, which meant the next move was his.

He reached for his hat and slipped her present out from where he'd tucked it inside his hat band. Holding it up, he let the moonlight catch on the bright beads.

"Momma and Belle go way back. Seems Belle finished my hatband after Momma passed. I asked her if she could make one for you. Turns out she already had while we were overseas."

"I don't have a hat." But she reached out to brush a finger across the beaded band in the moonlight. Even just by that she could tell it was beautiful work.

"I was thinkin' we could take care of that tomorrow afore we head out."

"Anything else you want to be a-changin', cowboy?" Her attempts at a Texas accent tickled him no end and she knew it.

"Depends on how you feel about wearing this as well?" He uncovered the end of the hatband tie that he'd been holding on to. The diamond on the ring of gold caught the moon and starlight, making it shine brighter than either one.

"Is that a proposal, cowboy?" Hannah's voice was only the softest whisper.

"Other than pushing you aside so that I can get up on one knee, it is, ma'am."

Again that silent study.

He waited her out. Then she reached for his phone. She typed in three more letters at the end of his message, before showing it to him.

We've accepted your suggestion to join Shadow Force: Psi.

"That's perfect."

She hit send and set the phone aside.

"Now, I'm still lying here waitin' on an answer to the other question of buying you a proper hat and all."

"And all," Hannah leaned down and kissed him.

Close by his right ear, he heard something whispered ever so softly.

Yes.

AT THE SOFTEST WORD

DON'T MISS THE CONTINUING STORY
(COMING SOON)

AT THE SOFTEST WORD (EXCERPT)

*R*icardo lay in the mud where the horse had tossed him and tried to ignore the cold rain slashing down on him. He still held his rifle securely in his hand, not that he had any live ammo for it. If he had to lie here much longer, he was going to club someone with it.

Just another day in Delta Force, he kept telling himself.

Except he wasn't in The Unit anymore.

This was all his Isobel's fault. Not the leaving The Unit part, but all the mud and rain part.

Why don't you all come up to Montana? And, like naive chumps, they all had. When the great film star Isobel Manella called, everyone came—even her twin brother. Which somehow meant that he'd ended up crawling through the near freezing mud.

One of the stuntmen on her movie had driven the thirty miles into the nearest town, gotten into a bar brawl with the locals last night, and was sleeping it off with one arm in a cast and the other handcuffed to a hospital bed.

Some Hollywood Joe-boy taking on a bar full of Montana ranchers—not the brightest dude.

Her director had needed five-ten of lean Latino dude about the same moment the Shadow Force's plane had landed…and he'd been volunteered.

If the fake rain that the water truck—clearly tapped directly from a glacial stream, maybe straight from a glacier itself—was using to pound him deeper into the cold mud didn't stop soon, he was definitely going to have to hurt someone. Not Isobel, of course. Not only was she the movie's star, but he'd long ago learned (probably while still in the womb) to never try to outsmart his twin.

Her skills as an empath had cut off every nefarious plan a twelve-minute-and-one-day younger twin brother could come up with before it even hatched—they'd split midnight between them and she'd been lording it over him ever since.

"You look so cute!" Michelle's voice bubbled into his brain. And there was his first target.

"Go to hell!" Telepathy had its uses; telling off Michelle Bowman was a good one.

"You wish. You do look seriously cute though, Manella. Great butt. Which is about all that's showing above the mud." She sent an emotion tag of *"(so laughing!)"* because their link passed no emotional intonation, just the words and timing.

He pushed himself up just enough that he could see her standing close behind the director. Even mixed into the crowd of male and female ranch hands gathered to watch the movie being made on their property, Michelle still stood out. Five-ten of sleek redhead in jeans, a flannel shirt, and cowboy boots—because, of course, she was always dressed perfectly for any occasion. She offered him one of her electric smiles.

He let himself drop back down into the mud. *Do not be thinking about that woman.* But telling himself off didn't help. And the cold mud wasn't enough of a distraction. To a former Unit operator, this was nothing. He'd take this any day over an Indonesian mangrove swamp crawling with eight kinds of nasties before you even started counting the critters that weren't carrying guns.

He began belly-crawling forward per the script.

Someone grabbed his hand, and it took all of his strength to not reflexively take them down hard. He was supposed to be a battle-battered hero after all.

Isobel, wearing the wet look like perfection, helped him to his feet. She slung his muddy arm over her denim-clad shoulder. At least they hadn't dressed her in one of those white blouses that went transparent when wet. His sister certainly had the figure for it and he liked that they hadn't taken the cheap shot. It saved him having to beat the shit out of the director.

"Remember to keep your head down. You look nothing like Javier," she whispered as he limped out of the mud straight toward the camera.

"Right. I'm much more handsome." He just wasn't the newest hot-guy movie star and Javier was.

His shirt, however, *was* paper-thin, torn in all the right places, and bloody—with more red leaking from the small bladder under his arm and trickling down his chest.

"I've got better pecs, too."

Ricardo could feel his sister's half laugh…

Available soon at fine retailers everywhere.

ABOUT THE AUTHOR

M.L. Buchman started the first of over 60 novels, 100 short stories, and an ever-growing pile of audiobooks while flying from South Korea to ride across the Australian Outback. All part of a solo around-the-world bicycle trip (a mid-life crisis on wheels) that ultimately launched his writing career.

Booklist recently named the start of one of M.L.'s series as "The Best 20 Romantic Suspense Novels: Modern Masterpieces." His military and firefighter series(es) have won Booklist "Top 10 Romance of the Year" 3 times. NPR and Barnes & Noble have named other titles "Top 5 Romance of the Year."

He has flown and jumped out of airplanes, can single-hand a fifty-foot sailboat, and has designed and built two houses. In between writing, he also quilts. M.L. is constantly amazed at what can be done with a degree in geophysics. He also writes: contemporary romance, thrillers, and SF. More info at: www.mlbuchman.com.

Other works by M. L. Buchman:

Short Story Series by M. L. Buchman:

The Night Stalkers
The Night Stalkers
The Night Stalkers 5E
The Night Stalkers CSAR
The Night Stalkers Wedding Stories

Firehawks
The Firehawks Lookouts
The Firehawks Hotshots
The Firebirds

Delta Force
Delta Force Short Stories

US Coast Guard
US Coast Guard

White House Protection Force
White House Protection Force Short Stories

Where Dreams
Where Dreams Short Stories

Eagle Cove
Eagle Cove Short Story

Henderson's Ranch
Henderson's Ranch Short Stories

Dead Chef Thrillers
Dead Chef Short Stories

Deities Anonymous
Deities Anonymouse Short Stories

SF/F Titles
The Future Night Stalkers
Single Titles

Printed in Great Britain
by Amazon